Mammals Contents

What Is a Mammal?

How are you like a zebra and a whale? You don't eat grass as a zebra does or live in the ocean with the whales. Zebras and whales are mammals. People are mammals, too. All mammals are alike in five important ways.

Mammals have hair on their bodies for part or all of their lives.

Mammals have large, well-developed brains that make them more intelligent than other kinds of animals.

Mother mammals nurse their babies, or feed them milk from the mothers' bodies.

Mammals are warm-blooded. The temperature of their bodies stays about the same no matter how warm or cool the weather.

Most mammals care for their young. They protect them and teach them the skills they will need to live on their own.

2

We're All Mammals

Mammals come in different sizes and shapes. Write the names of the mammals after their descriptions. Then find the names in the puzzle.

Elephant

Fox

Bat

Dolphin

Giraffe

Dog

1. I live in the ocean.

_____

2. You may think I'm a bird, but I'm not.

_____

3. I am a family pet.

_____

4. I am the tallest animal on Earth.

_____

5. I belong to the dog family, but I'm not a dog.

_____

6. I am the heaviest land animal.

_____

w	d	o	g	e	b	q	a
x	x	t	d	u	g	l	s
c	m	g	o	m	i	r	b
v	n	d	l	j	r	h	a
e	l	e	p	h	a	n	t
q	g	o	h	z	f	y	a
h	l	i	b	f	o	i
n	c	y	n	z	e	b	x

3

What Is a Mammal?

Mammal Bodies

The bodies of all mammals are alike in some ways. Every mammal has a **skeleton**, a frame of bones that supports and protects the body. Muscles are attached to the bones. Without muscles, animals wouldn't be able to move around.

All mammals have a heart and blood vessels that carry blood through the body. They have a stomach, lungs, brain, and many other organs, too.

Let's take a look inside the bodies of some mammals.

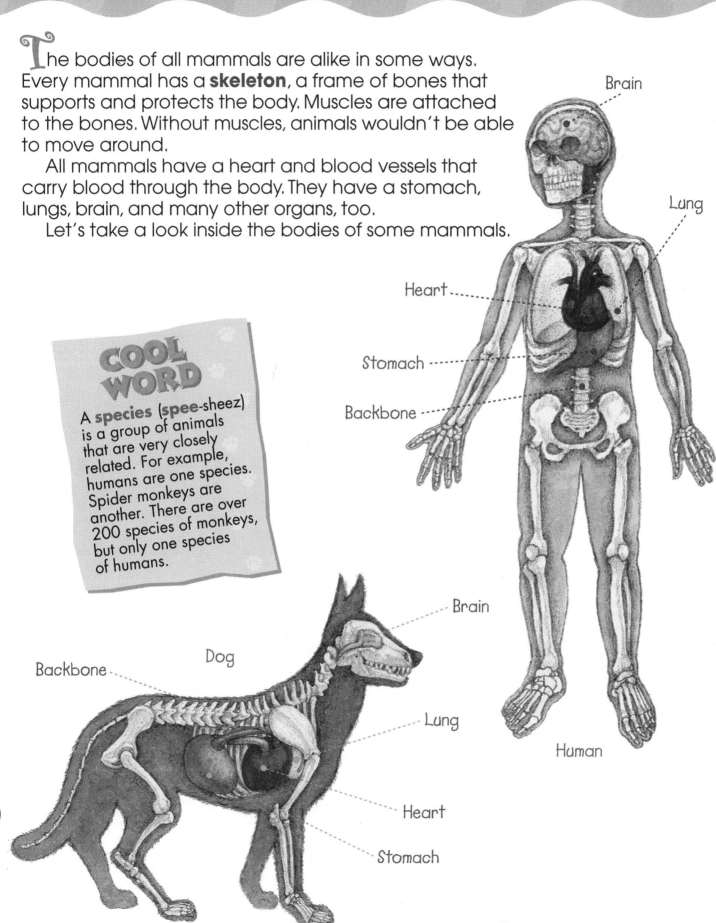

COOL WORD

A **species** (**spee**-sheez) is a group of animals that are very closely related. For example, humans are one species. Spider monkeys are another. There are over 200 species of monkeys, but only one species of humans.

Brain

Lung

Heart

Stomach

Backbone

Human

Brain

Dog

Backbone

Lung

Heart

Stomach

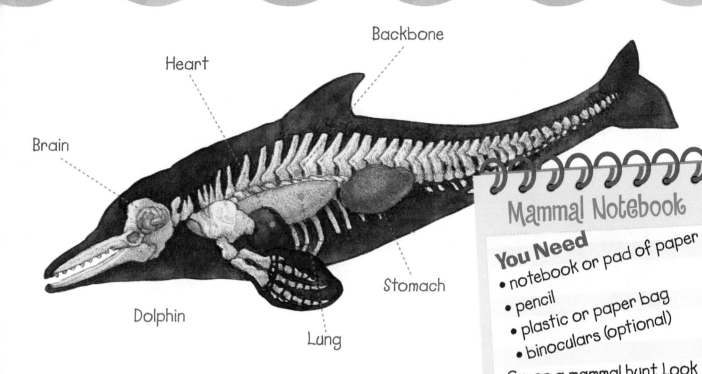

Backbone

Heart

Brain

Dolphin

Lung

Stomach

Mammals: True or False?

Write **true** or **false** after each sentence.

1. All mammals are warm-blooded. _____

2. All mammals have tails. _____

3. All mammals have many bones in their bodies. _____

4. All mammals have four legs. _____

5. All mammals have flippers. _____

6. All mother mammals nurse their babies. _____

7. All mammals have backbones. _____

8. All mammals have lungs and stomachs. _____

Which Ones Are Mammals?

Look at the animals. Write the name of each one in the correct column. Here's a challenge. For each animal that is not a mammal, explain what kind it is.

Sea Lion

Brown Bear

Mule Deer

Python

Hamster

Iguana

Monarch Butterfly

Llama

Mammal	Not a Mammal/Kind of Animal

Mammal Bodies

What Do Mammals Eat?

Most mammals eat plants. Plant-eating mammals, such as cows, have strong grinding teeth. Some animals eat meat only. Most animals that eat flesh must hunt for prey. They have sharp pointed teeth to catch and tear their food. Bears and skunks have teeth that grind and teeth that tear. They can eat both flesh and plants.

Mammals that hunt have good eyesight. Some see especially well at night. Their eyes are close together at the front of their heads. Hunted mammals, which usually eat plants, have widely spaced eyes.

COOL WORDS

Herbivores are animals that eat plants.
Carnivores are animals that eat flesh.
Omnivores are animals that eat plants and flesh.
What do you think animals that eat insects are called?

_____

Hunters and Hunted

List each animal in the correct column.

Fox

Cat

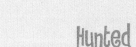

Squirrel

Rabbit

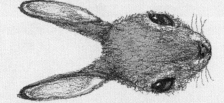

Wolf

Mouse

Hunters

_____

_____

_____

Hunted

_____

_____

_____

Awesome!

It's not hard to guess what anteaters eat, but do you know how they do it? They use their long, sticky tongues to lick up ants. Then they swallow the ants whole.

7

Mammals on the Move

You can find mammals in trees, under the ground, and in the air and water. But most mammals live on the ground.

Most mammals have four legs for walking, trotting, and galloping. Humans and gorillas have broad, flat feet that help them stand upright and run and walk on two legs.

Awesome!

Flying squirrels can't really fly. They glide.

Some mammals—rabbits and kangaroos are two examples—use their strong back legs to hop. Kangaroos' long, thick tails help them balance.

Many mammals that live in trees, such as monkeys, use their tails almost like extra legs or arms. Monkeys' hands, which have thumbs and fingers, help them grasp and swing, too.

Mammals that live in water have flippers instead of arms. Whales, dolphins, and other water mammals don't have legs at all.

Bats, the only mammals that fly, have wings instead of hands and arms.

Some small mammals, such as gophers and moles, spend most of their life underground. Moles' front legs face outward, which helps them "swim" through the soil.

How Do They Move?

Write the number of the word that describes the way each animal moves.

1. walks

2. swings

3. hops

4. gallops

5. flies

6. digs

Think of another mammal. Write its name and a word that describes the way it moves.

9

Mammals Attack

Most mammal hunters work alone. They hide and wait to jump out at their prey as it passes by. A male mountain lion hides at a water hole or trail waiting for prey. When a deer or elk passes by, the lion charges—often leaping as far as twenty feet. The lion uses its paw to snag the prey and kills it in just a few seconds.

COOL WORDS

Predators are animals that hunt other animals for food.
Prey are animals that are hunted.

Awesome!

The shrew, which is the size of a small mouse, has to eat its weight in food every day. This tiny but fierce fighter is almost blind. But it uses its sense of smell and its whiskers to track prey—usually insects, worms, and mice. The shrew's prey can be much bigger than the shrew!

Some hunters work together in groups. Wolves are the best example. A wolf by itself couldn't catch an animal larger than a deer. But a group of wolves take turns chasing prey until they wear it out. In this way a wolf pack can catch a 1,000-pound moose.

Mammals Defend Themselves

any mammals that are hunted find safety in groups. Muskoxen and bison form a circle around their calves to protect them. They face outward and crush predators with their hoofs.

Other animals rely on speed or camouflage. In summer, the snowshoe hare is brown, so the animal is well camouflaged in the forest. As winter comes, the hare sheds its coat and grows white fur.

Skunks defend themselves by lifting their tails and spraying stinky, stinging liquid into their enemies' faces.

Some animals, such as the tiny meadow vole, don't have any special defenses. They just have lots of babies to replace the ones that are eaten.

COOL WORDS

Bison (bye-sun) Most people call this animal a buffalo. But the bison has a bigger head and neck than buffaloes do. It also has humped shoulders and 14 pair of ribs, rather than the 13 that buffaloes have.
Camouflage (kam-uh-flahzh) is colors and markings that help animals blend with their surroundings.

A Sharp Defense

Use the code to fill in the letters and learn about another mammal defense.

			!						,
12	4	10	5	1	5	7	15	8	

1	6	11	3	3	9	4	11	16	16	1

8	15	12	6	2	10	6

									.
8	12	15	10	4	8	11	13	2	1

CODE

1 = S	9 = Q
2 = E	10 = C
3 = F	11 = I
4 = U	12 = O
5 = H	13 = N
6 = T	14 = H
7 = A	15 = R
8 = P	16 = L

11

Cold Places

Some mammals live in the Arctic where winters are long and dark. This far north, ice storms, blizzards, and temperatures way below zero are routine. How do mammals survive?

Polar bears have thick fur and layers of fat that keep them warm, even as they paddle through icy water with their strong front paws.

Walruses also have lots of fat, as well as tough, waterproof skin. Walruses have tusks, which they use to climb onto the ice and to fight. They use their strong, paddle-shaped front and back flippers to swim.

Cold Code

Cross off the letters **v**, **x**, and **y** to learn one reason walruses were important to the Inuit long ago and are still important to some Inuit today. Write the sentence on the lines.

xvyyIxxnvyuxvivytyyvxyyxyx xymvxavvdyyexvy
xvxwvyaxvlxxryyuvysvxy yyfxvayxtvyv yxixxnvyvtxvoxxv
vyoxxiyvlxvv yvytxyovvx vyxbxxuyxrvvnyyy xyivvnyxx
yyxlvxvayymvypXxsvxv xyayyynxvydvxv
vvvhyxveyyaxvtyxv vxhyvvoxxvuyvsxvexysxvyy.

_____

_____

Some mammals travel thousands of miles each year to find food or warmer weather. Many kinds of whales migrate to warm waters where they give birth. In summer, they travel to cold waters to feed.

Caribou are a kind of deer that live in far northern North America. They live in Europe and Asia, too, where they're called reindeer. At the end of each summer, herds of caribou travel south. They go to evergreen forests where they can find food. In spring, the herds return to their northern homes.

Awesome!

When caribou and deer migrate south, so do wolves that hunt them. The wolves need to stay close to their food.

Match the Mammals

Here are some mammals you've met on the last few pages. Draw lines to match them to their descriptions.

Watch out when I do this!

I'm tiny but tough.

I'm not always this color.

I'm a long-distance traveler.

I'm not afraid of a wolf, if it's by itself.

13

Mountains

High in the mountains the air is cold and hard to breathe, so mammals need warm fur and strong lungs. Sheep and goats that live in mountains have hoofs with sharp edges and rubbery bottoms to help them jump from ledge to ledge without slipping.

Some mountain mammals, the marmot is one, get fat during the summer and fall and **hibernate**, or sleep, during the winter. Hibernating mammals stay warm and don't need to eat very much.

Mountain & Arctic Mammals Puzzle

Fill in the sentences with words from the box. Then write the words in the puzzle.

walrus   hoofs   hibernate
fat   front   polar bear
skin   rubbery   fur   zero

Across

3. Layers of _____ help keep some mammals warm.

5. The white bear of the frozen Arctic is called the _____.

7. Walrus _____ is tough and waterproof.

9. The mountain goats' hoofs are _____ on the bottom.

10. The polar bear uses its _____ legs to pull itself through the water.

Down

1. A mammal with tusks that is related to seals is the _____.

2. Thick _____ keeps some mammals warm.

4. Mountain sheep and goats have sharp _____.

6. Some mammals sleep all winter, or _____.

8. In the Arctic, temperatures below _____ are not unusual.

Deserts

Deserts are the world's driest places. Days may be boiling hot and nights freezing cold. Some deserts are cold all the time. How do the mammals that live in these places cope?

Many desert animals are small. In the deserts of North America, kangaroo rats burrow into the ground. They get all the water they need from the seeds they eat. Larger desert animals, such as coyotes, hide under rocks and bushes when the sun is hot. In the Sahara Desert in North Africa, mammals hide from the sun during the day and come out in the evening to search for food.

Mammals at the Water Hole

Help the fennec fox and the dromedary camel get to the water hole.

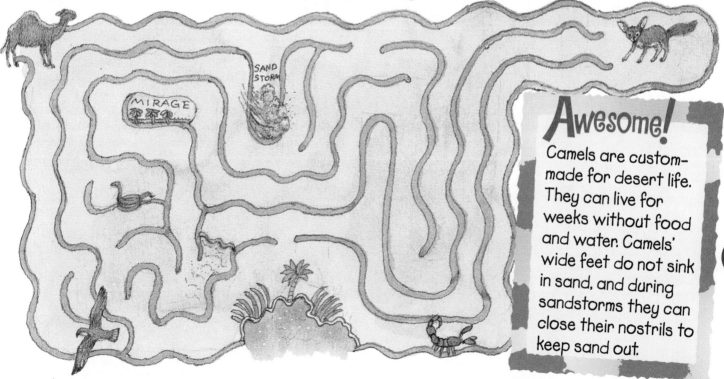

SAND STORM

MIRAGE

Awesome!

Camels are custom-made for desert life. They can live for weeks without food and water. Camels' wide feet do not sink in sand, and during sandstorms they can close their nostrils to keep sand out.

15

Forests

Forests around the world are homes to many mammals—large and small. Quite a few mammals, including otters, beavers, rabbits, deer, and bears, find food and places to live in the forests of North America.

How many animals do you see in the picture?

Log Jam

Help the beaver collect the logs with letters on them. Unscramble the letters to find out what a beaver's home is called.

d l g
d   g
e   o

☐ ☐ ☐ ☐ ☐

Making Tracks

You can identify mammals by their tracks. Beavers have webbed hind feet, and deer tracks look like upside-down hearts. Raccoon tracks look almost like human footprints. Look for tracks in the dirt and mud of forests. Match each type of tracks to the mammal that made it.

Raccoon

Beaver

Deer

Rabbit

Grasslands

Many mammals make their homes in grasslands, wide-open spaces dotted with bushes and trees. Africa has some of the most interesting grassland animals. Giraffes, zebras, lions, and elephants live in the open country of Africa.

Prairie dogs and bison live in North American grasslands. Kangaroos live in grasslands of Australia.

Awesome!

Cheetahs are great sprinters. They can run 65 miles an hour for short distances. That's as fast as the speed limit on many highways.

Stripes in the Grass

Camouflage helps many grassland mammals hide. Circle the mammals in the African grassland. How many can you find?

North American Grassland

I'm Lost!

Below are some other grassland animals. But they've forgotten where they live! Draw lines to put them in the African grassland or the North American grassland.

Hippopotamus

Jack Rabbit

Deer

African Grassland

Aardvark

Gnu

Coyote

19

Grasslands

Rain Forests

R ain forests, or jungles, of South America are very hot and steamy. Rain falls nearly every day. Lots of mammals live in rain forests. Some, such as sloths, spider monkeys, and howler monkeys, live in the treetops where there is sunlight and fruit to eat.

Jaguars stalk their prey on the jungle floor. But they can climb trees when they need to. Capybaras spend most of their time in rivers.

Which Mammal Am I?

Use the clues to write the name of each mammal. Then circle the names in the puzzle.

| tiger | coyote | camel |
| jaguar | beaver | raccoon |

j	a	g	u	a	r	x	y
o	r	a	c	c	o	o	n
c	t	f	o	r	p	a	q
a	i	p	y	p	g	s	x
m	g	q	o	w	m	a	g
e	e	q	t	o	k	l	f
l	r	b	e	a	v	e	r

1. I hide under bushes and rocks in the desert. Who am I?

   _____

2. I can live without food and water for weeks. Who am I?

   _____

3. My tracks look almost like footprints. Who am I?

   _____

4. My stripes help me hide in tall grasses. Who am I?

   _____

5. I stalk prey on the jungle floor and climb trees, too. Who am I?

   _____

6. My home is called a lodge. Who am I ?

   _____

In the Air

Most bats are **nocturnal**, or active at night. At dusk, many kinds of bats leave the dark caves in which they live to hunt for food. If you went into a bat cave during the day, you might see thousands of bats hanging upside down—fast asleep.

Brazilian Free-Tailed Bat

Dog-Faced Fruit Bat

Little Brown Bat

Trident
Leaf-Nosed Bat

Bat Chat

What do these coded sentences say?

CODE

8	10	11	5	2	6	7	9	3	4	1
e	d	v	i	l	r	m	b	a	o	p

I am a ☐☐☐☐☐☐☐ bat.
       11   3   7   1   5   6   8

I am the only bat that lives on the ☐☐☐☐☐
of animals.   9   2   4   4   10

Awesome!

The world's smallest mammal is a tiny bat. No bigger than a bumble-bee, the Kitti's hog-nosed bat weighs only a fraction of an ounce.

In Water

Oceans cover more than two-thirds of Earth's surface. Some mammals, including dolphins, porpoises, and whales, live their whole lives in oceans. Their streamlined bodies help them glide easily in their watery homes. They use their powerful tails to move forward and their flippers to steer and balance.

These animals breathe air through lungs as all mammals do. They come to the surface of the water to breathe out of a blowhole at the top of their head. This can cause a huge spout of water—as high as 50 feet for some whales.

Other mammals spend much, but not all, of their time in the water. These animals are more graceful in water than on land.

Awesome!

Two mammals are the world's largest animals. The blue whale, the largest animal of all, may be 100 feet long. That's longer than a tennis court! The blue whale may weigh 200 tons.

The biggest land animal, the African elephant, is about 13 feet tall and weighs about 12 tons.

How much longer is a blue whale than an elephant is tall?

_____

How much heavier is a blue whale than an African elephant?

_____

A Whale of a Puzzle

Fill in the blanks. Then write the words in the puzzle.

seals
steer
blowhole
water
surface
blue
walrus

Across

1. Whales use flippers to balance and _____.
2. Over two-thirds of Earth is covered by _____.
4. Dolphins breathe out a _____.
6. Sea lions and _____ spend much of their life in water.

Down

1. Porpoises come to the _____ to breathe.
3. The _____ whale is the largest animal on Earth.
5. The huge _____ spends lots of time in water.

Under the Ground

Gophers, moles, and similar burrowing mammals make underground homes. Rabbits live in **warrens**, holes in the ground connected by tunnels. Badgers' underground nests are called **sets**. Prairie dogs live under the ground in **colonies** or **towns**. As many as 500 prairie dogs may live in one colony.

Help Them Get Home

Help the rabbit find its way through the warren to its cozy nest. Then help the prairie dog get to its fluffy nest at the center of the colony. Which *mammal* has the shorter path?

Awesome! Prairie dogs kiss when they greet one another. That's how they tell their relatives from strangers.

24

Unusual Mammals

Australia is home to many interesting mammals. One group of mammals is called **marsupials**. Most marsupials develop in their mothers' pouches.

Kangaroos are the biggest marsupials, up to seven feet tall. About the size of a lima bean, a newborn kangaroo crawls into a pouch at the front of its mother's body. There it drinks its mother's milk and continues to grow. After a few months, the baby can leave the pouch for a while. But it continues to live in its mother's pouch for up to ten months more. Here are some other marsupials.

Awesome!

The opossum is the only marsupial that lives in North America.

Koala

Wombat

Another unusual Australian mammal is the platypus. The platypus has a hairless snout that looks like a duck's bill. Its wide, flat tail and webbed feet make it a good swimmer.

The platypus is one of the few mammals that lays eggs. Like other mammals, the babies drink their mother's milk.

Platypus

Marsupial Word Search

Circle the names of the marsupials.

wallaby
wombat
kangaroo
cuscus
koala
bandicoot

q	x	n	d	r	c	k	o	c
w	f	w	o	m	b	a	t	u
a	n	m	f	j	r	n	a	s
l	d	n	d	a	h	g	p	c
l	i	k	o	a	l	a	g	u
a	c	l	q	b	h	r	x	s
b	a	n	d	i	c	o	o	t
y	c	y	u	z	e	o	l	h

Mammals and People

$\mathcal{L}$ong ago, people trained some mammals to help them. Horses, donkeys, oxen, and elephants could carry heavy loads and pull plows. Some mammals were a source of food. Cows and goats gave milk. Pigs, cattle, and sheep provided meat. Tame animals, such as cows and pigs, are called **domesticated** animals.

Sort the Mammals

The picture shows some domesticated mammals and some wild mammals. List each mammal on the chart under Domesticated or Wild.

Domesticated	Wild

Dogs and cats are mammals that have been kept as pets by people all over the world for thousands of years. People provide food and shelter for their cats and dogs. In return, their pets are loyal, playful companions.

My Dog, Pal

Do you have a pet mammal? Fill in the questionnaire. If you don't have a pet mammal, describe a friend's—or describe an imaginary pet.

Name of pet: _____

Age: _____

Favorite food: _____
_____

A funny thing my pet does: _____
_____
_____

Why I like (or don't like) having my pet:
_____
_____
_____

Mammal Quiz

How well do you remember what you learned about mammals? Write **true** or **false** after each sentence. Look back at the page numbers in parentheses if you need help.

1. Mammals are warm-blooded. (Page 2)
_____

2. Some mammals have no skeleton. (Page 4)
_____

3. Mammals eat either plants or animals, but not both. (Page 7)
_____

4. Most mammals have four legs. (Page 8)
_____

5. Fur and fat help mammals live in cold places. (Page 12)
_____

6. Mammals that hibernate stay awake all winter. (Page 14)
_____

7. Many desert mammals hide from the sun during the day. (Page 15)
_____

8. No mammals lay eggs. (Page 25)
_____

Where Do Mammals Live?

Mammals live in many different kinds of home areas, or **habitats**, around the world. You can see some mammals and some of the places they live on the map.

North America

Atlantic Ocean

Pacific Ocean

South America

Africa

Place the Mammals

Do you know where the polar bear, llama, brown bear, giraffe, and kangaroo live? Draw lines from these animals to the parts of the world in which they live.

Arctic Ocean

Europe

Asia

Pacific Ocean

Indian Ocean

Australia

Answers

Page 3

1. dolphin
2. bat
3. dog
4. giraffe
5. fox
6. elephant

w	d	o	g	e	b	q	a
x	x	t	d	u	g	l	s
c	m	g	o	m	i	r	b
v	n	d	l	j	r	h	a
e	l	e	p	h	a	n	t
q	g	o	h	z	f	y	a
h	i	l	i	b	f	o	j
n	c	y	n	z	e	b	x

Page 7

insectivore

Hunters: fox, cat, wolf
Hunted: squirrel, rabbit, mouse

Page 12

Inuit made walrus fat into oil to burn in lamps and heat houses.

Page 15

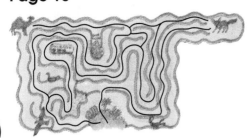

Page 5

1. true
2. false
3. true
4. false
5. false
6. true
7. true
8. true

Page 9

Answers will vary, but should include the name of a mammal and an action verb.

Page 13

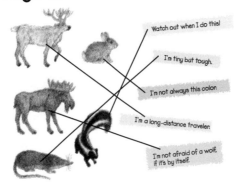

Watch out when I do this!

I'm tiny but tough.

I'm not always this color.

I'm a long-distance traveler.

I'm not afraid of a wolf, if it's by itself.

Page 16

There are seven hidden animals in the picture.

l o d g e

Page 6

Mammal
Brown Bear
Hamster
Mule Deer
Sea Lion
Llama

Not a Mammal/Kind of Animal
Monarch Butterfly/Insect
Iguana/Reptile
Python/Reptile

Page 11

OUCH! SHARP, STIFF QUILLS PROTECT PORCUPINES.

Page 14

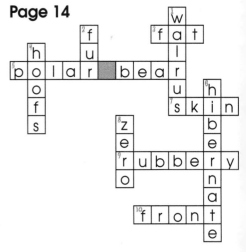

Page 17

Answers

Pages 18-19

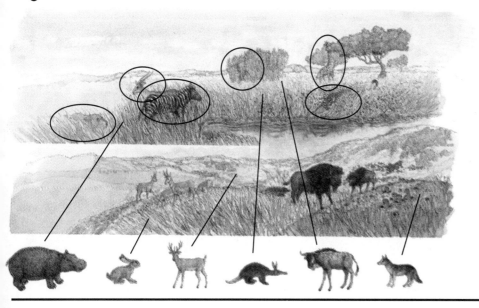

Page 20

1. coyote
2. camel
3. raccoon
4. tiger
5. jaguar
6. beaver

j	a	g	u	a	r	x	y
o	r	a	c	c	o	o	n
c	t	f	o	r	p	a	q
a	i	p	y	p	g	s	x
m	g	q	o	w	m	a	g
e	e	q	t	o	k	l	f
l	r	b	e	a	v	e	r

Page 21

vampire
blood

Page 22

87 feet
188 tons

Page 23

```
        1s  t  e  e  r
        u
        r
        f
     2w  a  t  e  r
  3b     c
4b  l  o  w  h  o  l  e
  u     5a
  e     l
        r
        u
     6s  e  a  l  s
```

Page 24

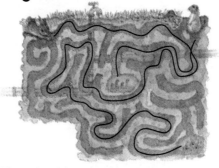

The prairie dog has the shorter path.

Page 25

q	x	n	d	r	c	k	o	c
w	f	w	o	m	b	a	t	u
a	n	m	f	j	r	n	a	s
l	d	n	d	a	h	g	p	c
l	i	k	o	a	l	a	g	u
a	c	l	q	b	h	r	x	s
b	a	n	d	i	c	o	o	t
v	c	y	u	z	e	o	l	h

Page 26

Domesticated:
cow
goat
horse
pig
dog
cat
sheep

Wild:
fox
rabbit
mouse
raccoon

Page 27

Pet questionnaire responses will vary.

1. true
2. false
3. false
4. true
5. true
6. false
7. true
8. false

Page 28

31

More About Mammals

Information Books

Elephants: Our Last Land Giants
by Dianne M. MacMillan

Mammals by David Burnie

Never Grab a Deer by the Ear
by Colleen Stanley Bare

Parenting Papas: Unusual Animal Fathers
by Judy Cutchins and Ginny Johnston

Tracks in the Wild by Betsy Bowen

Storybooks and Poetry

Another First Poetry Book compiled by Lucy Foster

Honey Paw and Lightfoot by Jonathan London

Stellaluna by Janell Cannon

Story of a Dolphin by Katherine Orr

Videotapes

The Arctic Region and Its Polar Bear
from Disney Educational Products

Bear Country from Disney Educational
Products

Dolphins: Our Friends from the Sea
from AIMS Media

Mammals from National Geographic

Small Animals of the Plains from Disney
Educational Products

Computer Software

Amazon Trail II MECC

Where in the World Is Carmen
Sandiego? Brøderbund

Toys and Games

Animals and How They Grow
A Wonders of Learning Kit from
National Geographic

Geo Safari, Animals of the World
Electronic game

Superdoodle Mammals Pattern
Activity book from The Learning Works

Magazines

International Wildlife

National Geographic World

Ranger Rick

Your Big Back Yard

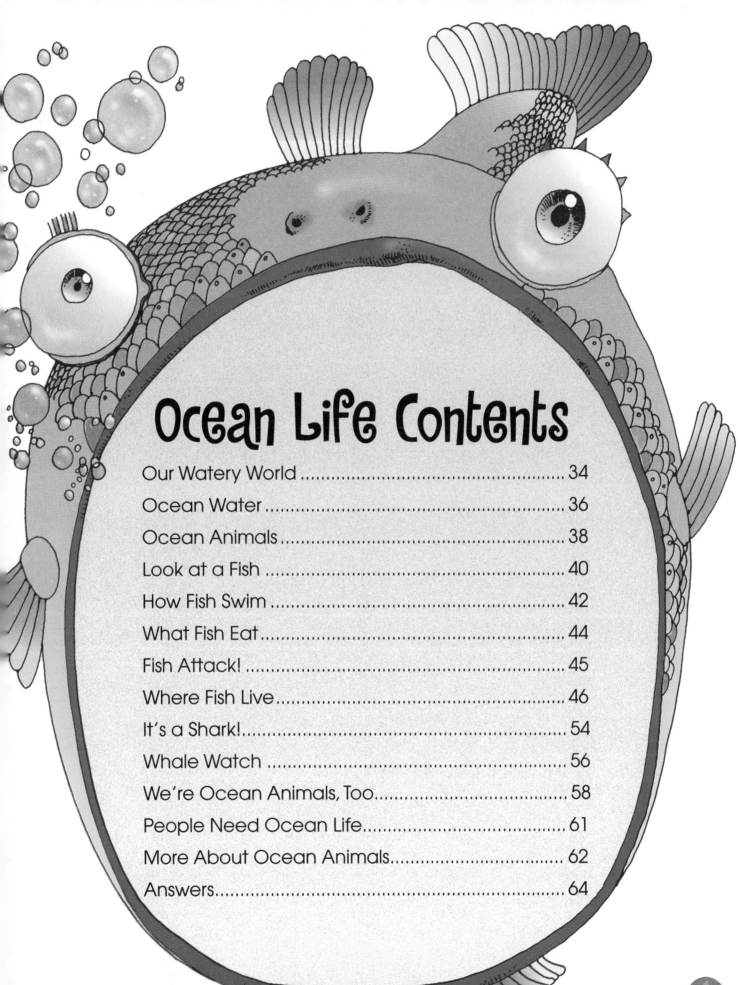

Ocean Life Contents

OUR WATERY WORLD

Wow! You're on the moon. See that blue-and-white marble in the black of space? It's Earth. The blue is water and the white swirls are clouds. Can you see small patches of brown and green? Those patches are land.

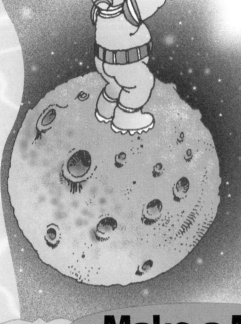

Make a Map

You need a blue crayon and a brown crayon.

1. Color the parts of the map labeled **W** blue.
2. Color the parts labeled **L** brown.

When you've finished coloring, stand up the book. Move back a few feet and squint your eyes as you look at the map. What do you notice about the blue parts of the map? That's right! They are all connected. That's why scientists say that there is really only one world ocean.

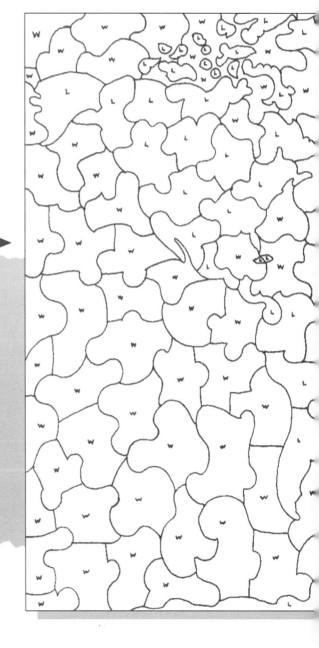

There is far more water than land on Earth. Almost three-fourths of Earth's surface is covered in water. And almost all of that water is in the ocean.

Write *water* and *land* on the right lines.

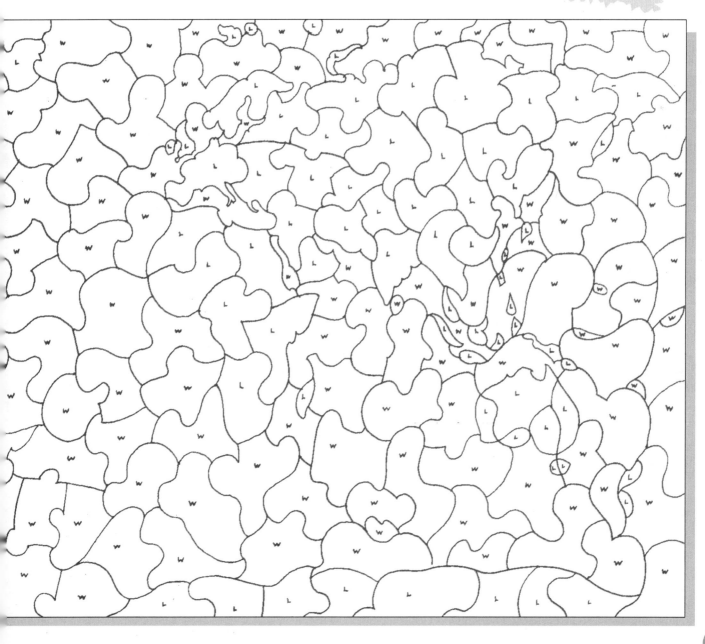

©1998 School Zone Publishing Company

Our Watery World

OCEAN WATER

Ocean water is different from the water in lakes and streams. Have you ever tasted ocean water? It's salty. Ocean water has the same kind of salt that you sprinkle on your food. The salt comes out of underwater volcanoes and rocks on the land. When it rains, the water wears away tiny bits of rocks and carries them in rivers to the ocean. After many millions of years, small amounts of salt add up to a very salty ocean.

AWESOME!

There is enough salt in the oceans to cover land with a layer over 500 feet thick.

Striped Blenny

Eel Grass

Sea Lettuce

Fiddler Crab

It's a Fact

Drinking salt water makes you even more thirsty. That's because people feel thirsty when their bodies need to get rid of salt.

Gas bubbles are in ocean water, too. The gases are the same as the ones in the air you breathe—oxygen, nitrogen, and carbon dioxide. Fish need the oxygen in water to breathe. Ocean plants produce the oxygen.

Sinking & Floating

Swimming in the ocean is different from swimming in a lake. Is it easier to float in salt water or fresh water? Try this activity to find out.

You need a clear jar or mug, an egg, warm water, salt, and a spoon.

1. Fill the bowl or mug halfway with warm water.

2. Gently place the egg in the water. Describe or draw what happens.

3. Take the egg out of the water. Add a spoonful of salt and stir until the salt disappears. (It's still there, but it has dissolved.)

4. Put the egg in the water again. What do you see?

Repeat steps three and four until you see a change.

From what you have observed, is it easier to float in the ocean or in fresh water?

_____

Earth's Oceans: True or False?

Write **true** or **false** after each sentence.

1. Fish need to breathe oxygen. _____

2. Not much of Earth's surface is covered by water. _____

3. All the oceans on Earth are connected. _____

4. The saltier the water is, the easier it is to float. _____

5. Water in lakes is salty. _____

See! You've already learned quite a bit about oceans.

Ocean Water

OCEAN ANIMALS

Close to shore or far from land, at the sunny surface or miles down in inky blackness, the ocean is filled with plants and animals. Most ocean animals are fish—about 20,000 different kinds. But other sorts of animals live in the ocean, too. Look at these ocean animals and the parts of the ocean where they live. Which of these animals are fish? It's not always easy to tell!

Seagulls

Flying Fish

Swordfish

Jellyfish

Halibut

Fish ID

Take a guess. Circle one of each kind of animal that you think is a fish. When you learn more about ocean life, turn back to this page to see whether you have changed your mind about any of the animals you identified.

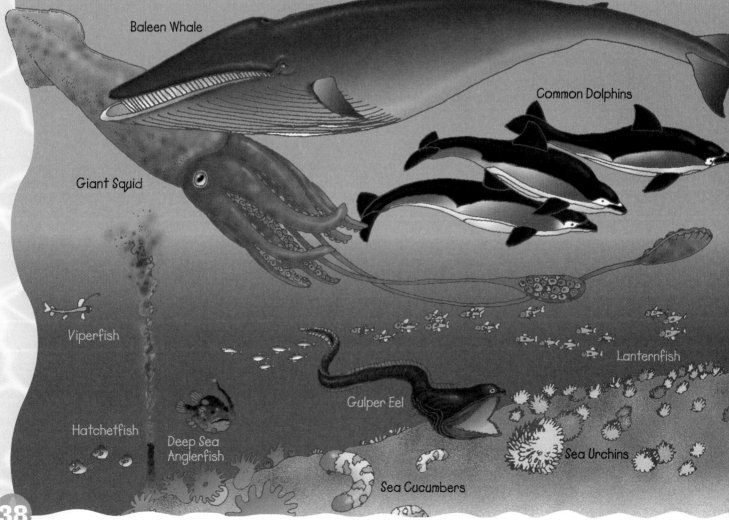

Baleen Whale

Common Dolphins

Giant Squid

Viperfish

Lanternfish

Gulper Eel

Hatchetfish

Deep Sea Anglerfish

Sea Urchins

Sea Cucumbers

Albatrosses

Sea Lions

Walruses

Mussels

Rockweed

TIDAL POOL

It's a Fact

Without sea plants there would be no animal life on Earth. The tiny ocean plants called algae (al-jee) make more than half of the world's oxygen, the gas needed for life.

OCEAN SURFACE

Tuna

Octopus

Skate

Cod

Killer Whale

Loggerhead Turtle

Anchovies

Humpback Whale

TWILIGHT WATERS

Manta Ray

Sea Pens

Anemones

Basking Sharks

Oysters

MIDNIGHT WATERS

Sponges

Tripodfish

Tubeworms

Ocean Animals

LOOK AT A FISH

What parts do nearly all fish have?

Motion Detectors
Fish can feel vibrations of the water that help them find other animals. Along the sides of their bodies and around each eye are openings that sense changes in water movement.

Scales
Most fish have hard scales covering their skin. A thin layer of slimy mucus covers the scales.

Jaw
Most fish have jaws with teeth that grab and bite.

Gill Slit
Fish use gills to get the oxygen they need from water. Water goes into the mouth, over the gills, and out through the gill slit. Oxygen moves through the gill into the fish's blood.

Fin
Almost all kinds of fish have fins. The fins on the sides are used for steering, stopping, and balancing. The fin on the tail is used for swimming.

Backbone
Fish have backbones inside their bodies.

Jaw

Rib

Spiny Fin Ray

Backbone Code

Use the code to finish the definition.

b	v	r	a	e	t	s
1	2	3	4	5	6	7

Animals with backbones are called

☐ ☐ ☐ ☐ ☐ ☐ ☐ ☐ ☐ ☐ ☐ .

2 5 3 6 5 1 3 4 6 5 7

The Name Game

These names are funny, but all four are names of real fish. Draw what you think these fish might look like. Be as silly or serious as you want.

Lionfish

Butterflyfish

Nurse Shark

Lemon Shark

Look at a Fish

HOW FISH SWIM

Most fish move forward by moving their tail fins as they curve their bodies from one side to the other. Fish "steer" with their side, or **pectoral**, fins. They stick out their left fin to turn left and their right one to turn right. To stop, they stick out both fins.

Fins Do It!

Which pilotfish is going faster? Why?

A

B

_____

_____

_____

_____

Herring are small fish that travel in groups, or **schools**, of thousands. The herring school is so tightly packed that it looks like one giant fish. Each herring stays in position by watching the fish to its left and right.

Some fish swim—and walk, too! A sculpin walks along the ocean floor on the tips of its side fins. A flying fish leaps out of the water to escape an enemy. It glides by stretching out its huge pectoral fins. A flight can last half a minute.

Flying Fish

Many fish can sink or rise when they want to. That's because they have pouches called **swim bladders** inside their bodies. Their swim bladders can fill up with gases and let out gases so the fish can float at any depth in the ocean. Without swim bladders, the fish would slowly sink to the bottom.

Make a Model Swim Bladder

How does a swim bladder work? Try this demonstration to find out.

You need a small plastic bottle with a tight-fitting cap, a sink, and water.

1. Fill the sink with water.

2. Fill the bottle with water. Tighten the cap.

3. Put the bottle in the water. Does it sink to the bottom?

4. Take away water from the "swim bladder" until it rises a bit. Keep pouring out water little by little until the bottle floats just below the surface of the water.

Air replaced the water you took out of the bottle. The more air that was in the "swim bladder" bottle, the higher it rose. That's how a swim bladder in a fish works, too.

Put Away Those Fish!

You know that the more air a fish has in its swim bladder, the higher it rises in the water. Write the number of each fish at the depth at which you might find it.

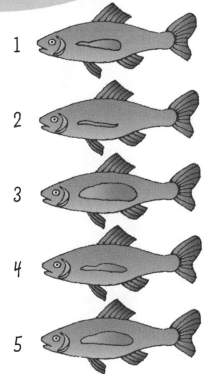

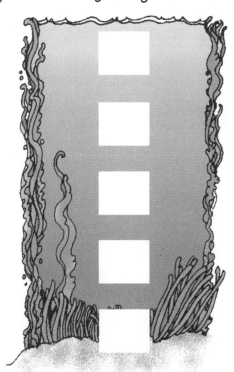

WHAT FISH EAT

Some parts of the ocean look more like soup than clear water. That's because the water contains millions of creatures called **plankton**. Many plankton are so tiny you'd need a microscope to see them. Plantlike plankton make their own food from sunlight. Other plankton are animals that eat the plantlike ones.

Fish eat plankton. Some fish eat smaller fish. A few fish eat others of their own kind. Who eats what or whom in the ocean is called a **food chain**.

Cod

Herring

Plantlike Plankton

Animal Plankton

Fish Food

GO!

To play Fish Food, you need a coin and one other player. One player is a whale shark and the other is a cod. Flip the coin. Heads goes first. Toss the coin. Heads moves one space; tails moves two. You get one point each time you land on a food your fish eats. The player with the most points at the end wins.

Plankton

Plankton

Tuna

Crab

Bottled-Nosed Dolphin

Herring

Plankton

Crab

Starfish

Plankton

Herrin

What Fish Eat

FISH ATTACK!

Ocean animals have many ways to attack and defend themselves, from great speed and a super sense of smell to electric shock and thick clouds of brown ink.

Sharks have huge jaws stuffed with sharp, pointed teeth. As their teeth wear out, they have several rows ready to replace them.

When the porcupine fish is attacked, it gulps water and blows itself up into a ball. Spines on its side stick out, making the fish a prickly mouthful.

If a fish comes too close, the sea cucumber shoots out sticky strands that trap the fish and give the sea cucumber time to escape.

The dragonfish has brilliant warning colors. Any animal that comes too close to its fins is jabbed with poison-filled spines. The stonefish hides on the ocean floor and injects prey with poison from its needlelike spines.

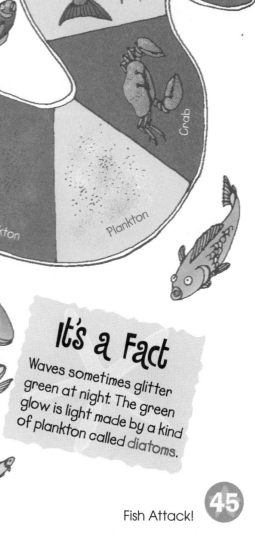

STOP!

Tuna

Crab

Plankton

Sea Cucumber

Plankton

Plankton

Crab

Nurse Shark

Herring

Herring

Clownfish

WHERE FISH LIVE

Close to Shore

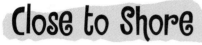

Fish live in all parts of the ocean. The greatest number of fish live in the shallow water over the continental shelf, the land that slants down from the edge of the continents.

Tidal Pools

A tide is something like a wave, except that waves are moved by wind along the top of the water, and tides move from the floor and middle of the ocean, too. Tides are caused mainly by the pull of gravity from the moon. After a few hours at the beach, you'll realize that part of the beach is under water. That's the tide coming in. In a few more hours the water will move out again.

Pockets of water called **tidal pools** are left in rocky places on shore when the tide goes out. There's lots of life in tidal pools. Plants and animals have the food, clean water, and sunlight they need to live and grow. But they must be able to stand changes in water temperature and the pounding of waves.

Kelp

Clingfish

Brown Seaweed

Mussels

Goby

Limpets

Green Crab

Periwinkles

Starfish

Plant or Animal?

Can you tell whether some of the living things in a tidal pool are plants or animals? Take a guess. Write the name of each living thing in the tidal pool under **Plants** or **Animals**. Check the answer page to see if you are right.

Plants

_____
_____
_____
_____
_____
_____
_____
_____

Animals

_____
_____
_____
_____
_____
_____
_____
_____
_____
_____
_____
_____

Bladder Wrack

Knotted Wrack

Sea Lettuce

Sugar Kelp

Barnacles

Anemones

Sea Snails

Where Fish Live

Coral Reefs

Look for coral reefs in warm, shallow ocean waters. The reefs grow on top of the skeletons of tiny animals called **polyps**. Coral reefs are home to lots of very colorful fish.

KEY

Coral Reefs

Moray Eel

Reef Shark

Clownfish

Grouper

Butterflyfish

Staghorn Coral

Stoplight Parrotfish

Lionfish

Squirrelfish

Seafan

It's a Fact
The Great Barrier Reef off the coast of Australia is the largest coral reef in the world. It stretches for over 1,200 miles and can be seen from the moon.

Giant Clam

Brain Coral

Spotted Starfish

Anemones

Sponges

Where Fish Live

Fish Homes Puzzle

Use the clues to fill in the puzzle.

Across

3. places off a coast where seaweed grows as tall as trees
6. a fish that doesn't look like one
8. Seaweed doesn't have ___ to take in water.
9. You'll find the most colorful fish here.

Down

1. These form when wind blows across the ocean.
2. a fish that looks like its name and stays near the ocean floor
4. When the tide goes out, ocean water is left here.
7. The moon causes the ___ .
5. Skeletons of these tiny animals form coral reefs.

AWESOME!

Cleaner wrasse clean the teeth and pick the dead skin and little animals from larger fishes' bodies. Even when they swim right into a mouth filled with sharp teeth, the tiny fish are in no danger.

waves

coral reefs   roots

kelp forests   seahorse

tides   tidal pools

rockfish

polyps

Where Fish Live

Far from Shore

Scientists divide the open ocean far from land into three layers according to how much sunlight the water gets: the sunlight zone, the twilight zone, and the midnight zone.

Sunlight Zone

The sunlight zone is the ocean's top layer. It goes down about 300 feet, and the temperature is a pleasant 70° F. Even though it is the smallest zone, it has about 90 percent of ocean life. Sunlight brightens the water near the surface where plankton float. Bigger creatures also live in the sunny water. Some swimming animals cruise just below the surface. Some dive deep. Others break the water's surface to reach the air above.

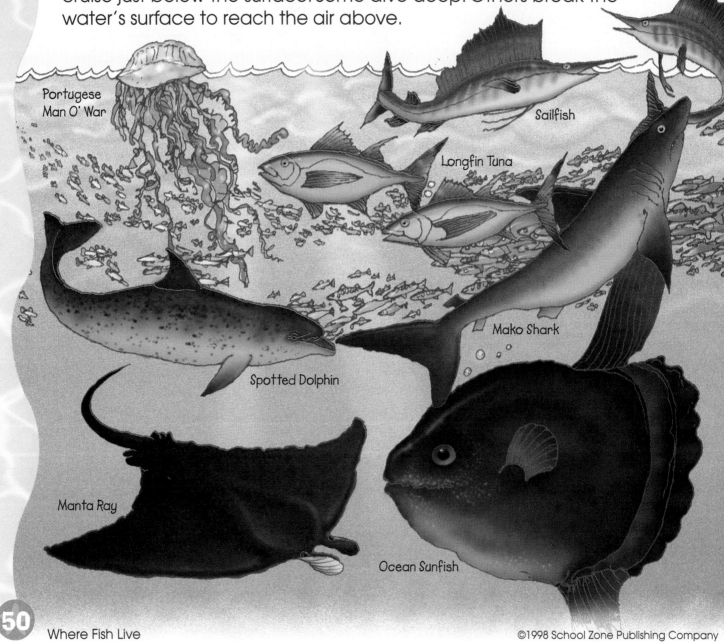

Portugese Man O' War

Sailfish

Longfin Tuna

Mako Shark

Spotted Dolphin

Manta Ray

Ocean Sunfish

Twilight Zone

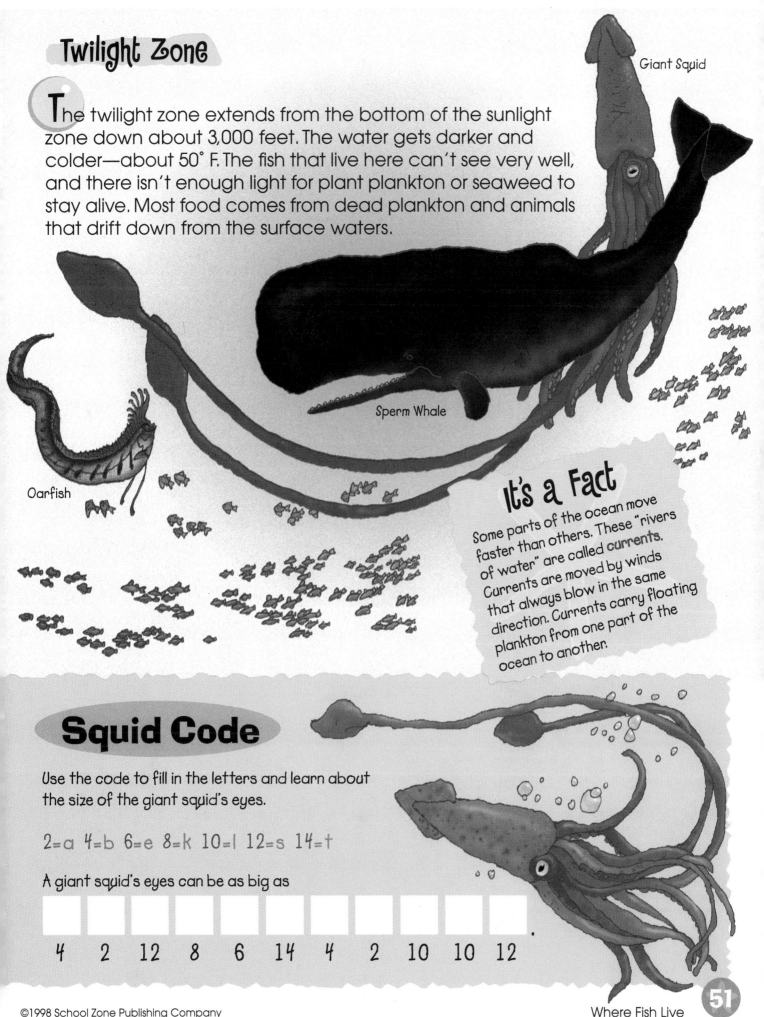

Giant Squid

The twilight zone extends from the bottom of the sunlight zone down about 3,000 feet. The water gets darker and colder—about 50° F. The fish that live here can't see very well, and there isn't enough light for plant plankton or seaweed to stay alive. Most food comes from dead plankton and animals that drift down from the surface waters.

Sperm Whale

Oarfish

It's a Fact

Some parts of the ocean move faster than others. These "rivers of water" are called currents. Currents are moved by winds that always blow in the same direction. Currents carry floating plankton from one part of the ocean to another.

Squid Code

Use the code to fill in the letters and learn about the size of the giant squid's eyes.

2=a 4=b 6=e 8=k 10=l 12=s 14=t

A giant squid's eyes can be as big as

4	2	12	8	6	14	4	2	10	10	12

Midnight Zone

The midnight zone goes from the bottom of the twilight zone to the floor of the ocean. This zone is dark and still. The temperature is really cold—about 43° F. The weight of the water from above presses very hard on the small, nearly blind animals that live here. Many deep-ocean fish have parts that glow from chemicals in their bodies. Their lights confuse enemies, lure prey, and attract mates.

At some places on the ocean floor, water as hot as 750° F shoots out of openings, or **vents**. Minerals collect around the vents to form underwater chimneys. The hot water rising from the chimneys looks like black smoke.

Shrimp

Devilfish

Ratfish

Clams

Sea Urchin

AWESOME!

The very deepest parts of the ocean are cracks in the ocean floor called trenches. You could stack up to 26 Empire State Buildings and drop them into the deepest trench.

Three of these fish are in the wrong zones.
Circle them and draw a line from each circle
to the zone in which each fish lives. Look at pages 38,39,50,51, and 52 for help.

Rezone the Fish

SUNLIGHT WATERS

TWILIGHT WATERS

MIDNIGHT WATERS

Giant Tube Worms

Deep Sea Anglerfish

Sea Spider

What Do You Think?

Fish in the deepest water are usually small. Most of them have very big mouths. Why might they look like this? Write your ideas.

_____
_____
_____
_____
_____
_____
_____
_____

Where Fish Live

IT'S A SHARK!

Sharks have terrible reputations. It's true that a few kinds of sharks, such as great white sharks, attack swimmers. But most sharks stay far away from people. Some of the hundreds of kinds of sharks are far too small—as small as five inches long—to hurt humans. Others are huge—as long as forty feet. Most sharks eat meat, and often that meat is other sharks.

Sharks are fish, but they don't have bones. Instead, a shark's skeleton is made of the same material as the tip of your nose and your ears.

Sharks have streamlined bodies that help them glide through the water easily.

Sharks use their great hearing, vision, and sense of smell to hunt for food. They also use a sense that you don't have. All animals send out a little bit, or field, of electricity. Sharks sense this electricity through special tubes in their heads.

- Tail

Second Dorsal Fin

Pectoral Fin

COOL WORDS

The rubbery material that a shark's skeleton is made of is called **cartilage**. The shark's tiny, tooth-shaped scales are called **denticles**.

A-Mazing Sharks

A bull shark may swim from the ocean into a river or lake. Help this bull shark find its way back to salt water.

Tiger Shark

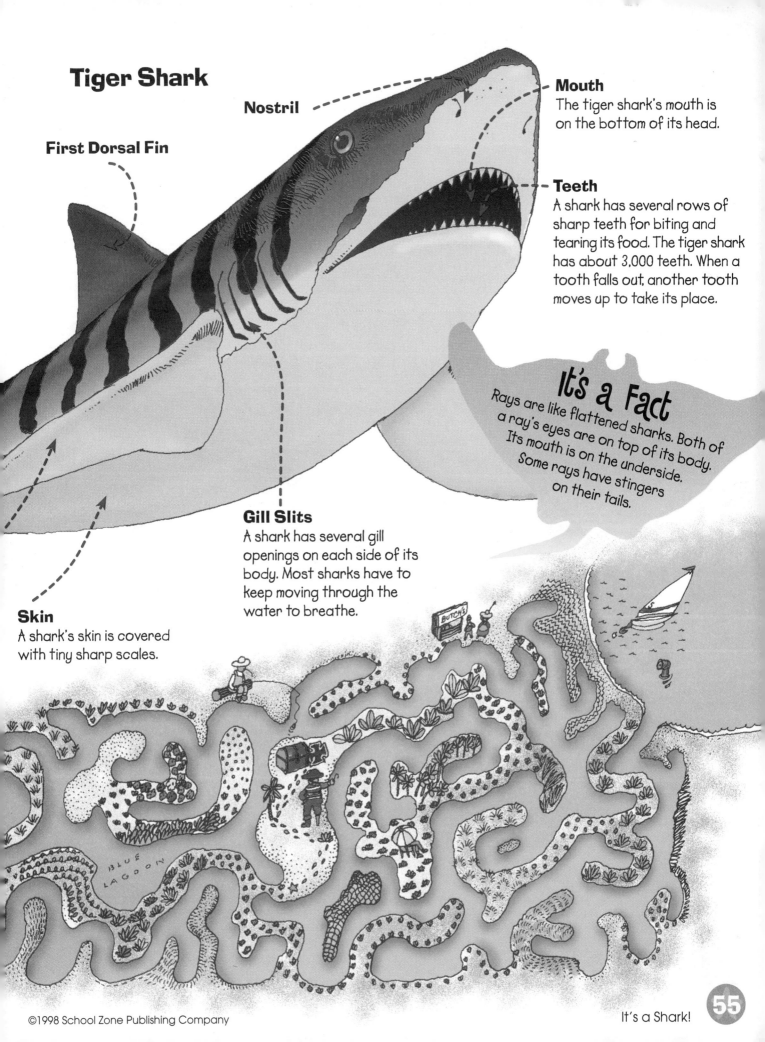

Nostril

First Dorsal Fin

Mouth
The tiger shark's mouth is on the bottom of its head.

Teeth
A shark has several rows of sharp teeth for biting and tearing its food. The tiger shark has about 3,000 teeth. When a tooth falls out, another tooth moves up to take its place.

It's a Fact
Rays are like flattened sharks. Both of a ray's eyes are on top of its body. Its mouth is on the underside. Some rays have stingers on their tails.

Gill Slits
A shark has several gill openings on each side of its body. Most sharks have to keep moving through the water to breathe.

Skin
A shark's skin is covered with tiny sharp scales.

BUTCH'S

BLUE LAGOON

55

It's a Shark!

WHALE WATCH

Whales and dolphins may look like fish, but they are actually huge mammals. The blue whale is the largest animal on Earth—100 feet long and 150 tons. That's as long as three railroad cars and as heavy as 30 African elephants!

Like all mammals, whales give birth to live young and feed their babies with milk from the mother's body. They breathe air through lungs, and they are warm-blooded. Their large brains make them smart.

Fluke
A whale travels by moving its flukes up and down, not side to side as a fish does.

Blowhole
A whale breathes through a blowhole at the top of its head. A huge cloud of moisture shoots out the blowhole when it breathes out.

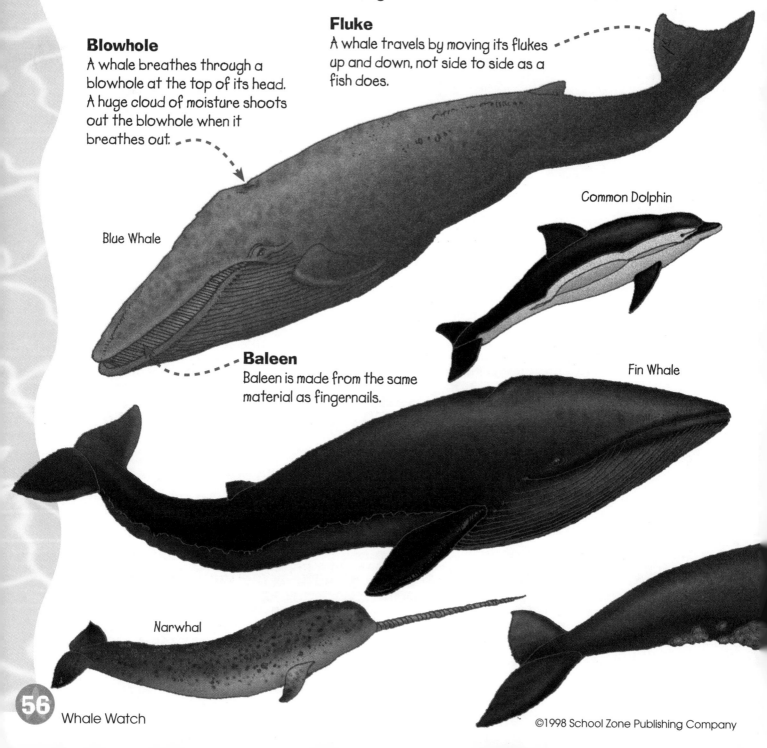

Common Dolphin

Blue Whale

Baleen
Baleen is made from the same material as fingernails.

Fin Whale

Narwhal

Whales' bodies are suited to life in the ocean. Their streamlined bodies and smooth, rubbery skin help them slip easily through water. Whales can hold their breath a lot longer than you can. A sperm whale can wait 75 minutes between breaths.

There are two kinds of whales. Baleen whales have lots of thin plates called **baleen** in their mouths through which they strain plankton from the water. Toothed whales use their teeth to capture prey, but they don't chew it up. They swallow their prey whole. Dolphins and porpoises are two kinds of toothed whales.

COOL WORD
Warm-blooded animals have body temperatures that stay about the same no matter what the temperature of the water or air.

Whales: Big, Bigger, Biggest

Use the whale graph to answer the questions.

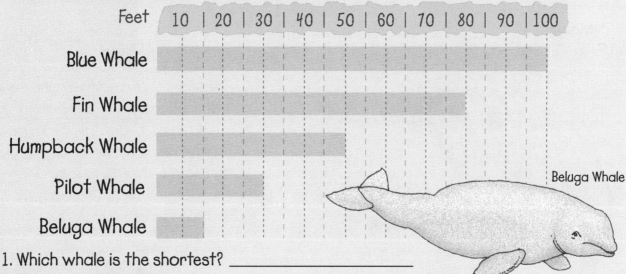

Feet	10	20	30	40	50	60	70	80	90	100
Blue Whale										
Fin Whale										
Humpback Whale										
Pilot Whale										
Beluga Whale										

Beluga Whale

1. Which whale is the shortest? _____

2. Which whale is 80 feet long? _____

3. How much longer is the humpback whale than the pilot whale? _____

4. What is the difference in feet between the longest and shortest whale? _____

It's a Fact
Seals, sea lions, and walruses are ocean mammals, too. But unlike whales, they spend part of their lives on land.

Black Right Whale

WE'RE OCEAN ANIMALS, TOO

Jellyfish, Octopuses, and More

Quite a few ocean animals are **invertebrates**, animals without backbones.

Arm

Mouth

Jellyfish look like clear, floating umbrellas. Not only do they lack a skeleton, they have no brain. All animals must watch out for a painful sting from the jellyfish's trailing arms, or tentacles.

Tube Foot

Mouth

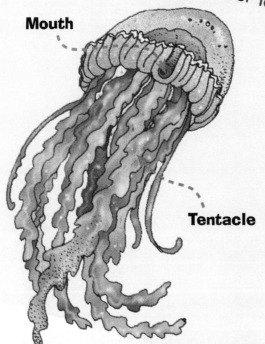

Tentacle

The starfish is a spiny-skinned animal with pointed arms and a mouth and stomach at the middle of its body. It moves around using its tiny tube feet. Starfishes' arms can drop off if something grabs them. Don't worry—the arms grow back.

Tail

Antenna

Leg

Lobsters have hard shells on the outside of their bodies. Lobsters have to **molt**, or shed their shells, to grow. Do you think lobsters are red? That's **after** they are cooked. Most kinds of lobsters are dark green or blue with spots. Lobsters are covered with tiny hairs that can sense the chemicals animals give off. That's how they find their food. They often eat animals that are related to them, including crabs and shrimp.

Eye

Claw

We're Ocean Animals, Too

Like jellyfish, octopuses have tentacles, eight long arms with suckers on the bottom. They can creep along on their arms, but octopuses have a quicker way to travel—by jet propulsion. The octopus sucks water into its body and shoots it out through a narrow opening. The force of the water moves the octopus forward rapidly.

Eye

Tentacle

Sucker

AWESOME!

A starfish eats when it takes its stomach out to lunch! The stomach comes out of the mouth in the middle of the underside, gets inside a clam shell, and slowly digests the clam.

Who Am I?

Write the number to match each clue with the animal it describes.

1. My eyes are at the end of long stalks.

2. My mouth and stomach are in the same part of my body.

3. I float on top of the water like an umbrella.

4. I can move really fast—but not as fast as a jet.

We're Ocean Animals, Too

Ocean Birds

Kittiwake

Tern

Lots of kinds of birds depend on the ocean for food. Some, such as pelicans, cormorants, and seagulls, stay along the coasts, and others hunt for food close to shore. Some offshore birds are penguins, puffins, and terns. You'll find albatrosses, petrels, and kittiwakes miles out over the open ocean.

Cormorant

Seagull

Pelican

Petrel

Penguin

Albatross

Bird Word Search

Circle the names of these nine sea birds in the puzzle.

A	P	E	L	I	C	A	N	W
K	L	D	F	J	O	S	W	P
I	C	B	Q	P	R	M	S	E
T	S	W	A	E	M	O	F	N
T	E	R	N	T	O	G	K	G
I	A	D	U	R	R	W	M	U
W	G	S	I	E	A	O	Q	I
A	U	Y	F	L	N	Q	S	N
K	L	J	F	U	T	B	X	S
E	L	P	U	F	F	I	N	Q

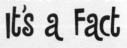

Puffin

It's a Fact

The albatross is the biggest sea bird. Its long narrow wings are about twelve feet across. The shape and length of its wings help the albatross soar and glide in the strong winds over the open ocean.

We're Ocean Animals, Too

PEOPLE NEED OCEAN LIFE

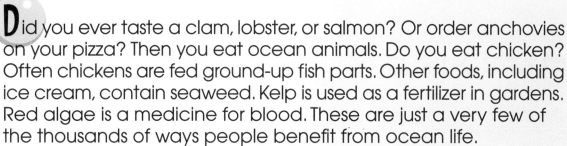

Did you ever taste a clam, lobster, or salmon? Or order anchovies on your pizza? Then you eat ocean animals. Do you eat chicken? Often chickens are fed ground-up fish parts. Other foods, including ice cream, contain seaweed. Kelp is used as a fertilizer in gardens. Red algae is a medicine for blood. These are just a very few of the thousands of ways people benefit from ocean life.

People put things in the ocean that can harm fish and other ocean life. The worst kinds of ocean pollution are from human and animal waste (the kind you flush away) and chemicals. Garbage, including plastic bags and six-pack rings, often finds its way into the ocean. Ocean animals may eat plastic bags or get their heads caught in the rings of six-packs. What can you do? Most important, don't litter!

What a Mess!

Sometimes oil tanker ships leak oil onto the surface of the ocean. Currents and tides can carry the pollution from the ship. Ocean animals that get coated with the oil may die. Can you find a good way to clean up oil spills?

You need a small plastic container with a lid, water, vegetable oil, and sand or pebbles.

1. Put sand or pebbles in the bottom of the container—that's your beach.

2. Pour in a little water so that part of the beach is still dry.

3. Add a spoonful of vegetable oil—that's the oil spill.

4. Gently rock the container back and forth. The movement of the water is like waves at the shore. What happens to the dry beach?

5. Now think of ways to clean the oil from the beach and water. Try out your best idea and write about how it worked.

©1998 School Zone Publishing Company   People Need Ocean Life

MORE ABOUT OCEAN ANIMALS

Information Books

The Magic School Bus on the Ocean Floor
by Joanna Cole

Watch Out for Sharks! by Caroline Arnold

The Desert Beneath the Sea by Ann McGovern
and Eugenie Clarke

Night Reef: Dusk to Dawn on a Coral Reef
by William Sargent

The Aquarium Book by George Ancona

The Aquarium Take-Along Book
by Sheldon L. Gerstenfeld

Outside and Inside Sharks by Sandra Markle

Sharks by Gail Gibbons

Safari Beneath the Sea by Diane Swanson

Storybooks

Shark in the Sea by Joanne Ryder
The Birth of a Whale by John Archambault
The Rainbow Fish by Marcus Pfister
The Sea and I by Harutaka Nakawatari
A House for Hermit Crab by Eric Carle

Organizations

American Zoo and Aquarium Association, Bethesda, MD

Center for Marine Conservation, Washington, DC

Cousteau Society, Norfolk, VA

Magazines

Chickadee

Owl

Ranger Rick

Your Big Backyard

National Geographic World

Wild Outdoor World

Aquariums

Tennessee Aquarium, Chattanooga, TN

Florida Aquarium, Tampa, FL

New England Aquarium, Boston, MA

Mystic Aquarium, Mystic, CT

New York Aquarium, New York, NY

National Aquarium, Baltimore, MD

Aquarium of the Americas, New Orleans, LA

John G. Shedd Aquarium, Chicago, IL

Vancouver Aquarium, Vancouver, Canada

Seattle Aquarium, Seattle, WA

Oregon Coast Aquarium, Newport, OR

Steinhart Aquarium, San Francisco, CA

Monterey Bay Aquarium, Monterey, CA

Stephen Birch Aquarium Museum, La Jolla, CA

Sea World, Orlando, FL; Tampa, FL; San Diego, CA

More About Ocean Animals

ANSWERS

Page 34

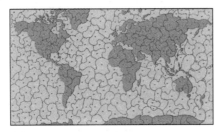

Pages 38-39

Fish:

Flying Fish	Gulper Eel
Swordfish	Basking Sharks
Tuna	Viperfish
Skate	Hatchetfish
Cod	Lanternfish
Anchovies	Tripodfish
Halibut	Manta Ray
Deep Sea Anglerfish	

Page 47

Plants

Kelp
Brown Seaweed
Bladder Wrack
Knotted Wrack
Sugar Kelp
Sea Lettuce

Animals

Limpets
Periwinkles
Starfish
Green Crab
Mussels
Clingfish
Goby
Anemone
Barnacles
Sea Snails

Page 54

One of several possible paths through
the maze is shown.

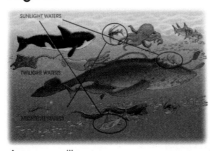

Page 35

land
water

Page 41

v	e	r	t	e	b	r	a	t	e	s
2	5	3	6	5	1	3	4	6	5	7

Page 42

Pilotfish **A** fish is going faster
because its fins are close to
its body.

Page 49

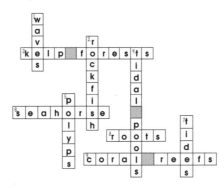

Page 53

Answers will vary.

Page 37

in the ocean
1. true
2. false
3. true
4. true
5. false

Page 43

3
5
1
4
2

Page 51

b	a	s	k	e	t	b	a	l	l	s
4	2	12	8	6	14	4	2	10	10	12

Page 57

1. beluga whale
2. fin whale
3. 20 feet
4. 85 feet

Page 59

Page 60